WHAT DO THEY DO?

WHAT DOES THE MAYOR DO ALL DAY?

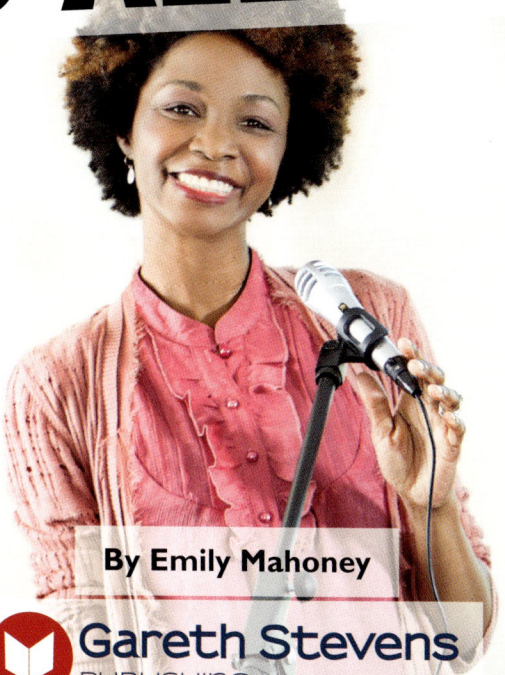

By Emily Mahoney

Please visit our website, www.garethstevens.com. For a free color catalog of all our high-quality books, call toll free 1-800-542-2595 or fax 1-877-542-2596.

Library of Congress Cataloging-in-Publication Data

Names: Mahoney, Emily Jankowski, author.
Title: What does the mayor do all day? / Emily Mahoney.
Description: New York : Gareth Stevens Publishing, [2021] | Series: What do they do? | Includes bibliographical references and index. | Contents: Being in charge – Getting elected – Meetings – Making decisions – Giving a speech – Exciting events – A position of power.
Identifiers: LCCN 2020003542 | ISBN 9781538256817 (library binding) | ISBN 9781538256794 (paperback) | ISBN 9781538256800 | ISBN 9781538256824 (ebook)
Subjects: LCSH: Mayors–Juvenile literature. | Municipal government–Juvenile literature.
Classification: LCC JS141 .M34 2021 | DDC 352.23/2160973–dc23
LC record available at https://lccn.loc.gov/2020003542

Published in 2021 by
Gareth Stevens Publishing
111 East 14th Street, Suite 349
New York, NY 10003

Copyright © 2021 Gareth Stevens Publishing

Editor: Emily Mahoney
Designer: Laura Bowen

Photo credits: Series art Dima Polies/Shutterstock.com; cover, pp. 1, 7 SDI Productions/E+/Getty Images; p. 5 Jupiterimages/PHOTOS.com/Getty Images Plus/Getty Images; p. 9 Martin Barraud/OJO Images/Getty Images; p. 11 monkeybusinessimages/iStock/Getty Images Plus/Getty Images; p. 13 Jacobs Stock Photography Ltd/Digital Vision/Getty Images; p. 15 sturti/E+/Getty Images; pp. 17, 21 Hill Street Studios/Digital Vision/Getty Images; p. 19 GregorBister/E+/Getty Images.

All rights reserved. No part of this book may be reproduced in any form without permission in writing from the publisher, except by a reviewer.

Printed in the United States of America

Some of the images in this book illustrate individuals who are models. The depictions do not imply actual situations or events.

CPSIA compliance information: Batch #CS20GS: For further information contact Gareth Stevens, New York, New York, at 1-800-542-2595.

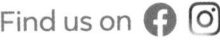

CONTENTS

Being in Charge. 4

Getting Elected. 6

Meetings. 8

Making Decisions. 12

Giving a Speech. 16

Exciting Events 18

A Position of Power 20

Glossary. 22

For More Information. 23

Index 24

Boldface words appear in the glossary.

Being in Charge

Being the mayor of a town or city is an important and special job. The mayor helps to make decisions for the town. They are also in charge of **departments** such as police and fire. But what does an actual day look like for the mayor? Read on to find out!

Getting Elected

Before a mayor can start working, they need to be **elected**. This means that people must choose them to do this important job. The candidate, or person who wants to be mayor, must have a plan that says what they will do to help their city or town if they are elected.

Meetings

Once a mayor is elected, they have a big job to do! One common thing a mayor does is to meet with the heads of different departments in the town, such as **transportation** or police. They check on how things are being run. **Communication** is an important part of keeping a town running smoothly!

Sometimes, the mayor also gets the opportunity to meet with people who live in the town. The mayor can listen to any concerns or problems that the **residents** are having so that they can learn how to make the town better. These meetings are important because it gives people in town a chance to say what they think.

Making Decisions

The mayor is commonly responsible for making many decisions for the town. Sometimes, these decisions are made into laws. They can also be about smaller things, such as whether or not to build a new park or get new supplies for the town library.

The mayor might have to decide who to **hire** for a certain job or position. The mayor often has the final say in choosing people for important jobs within the town's departments. The candidate might **interview** with the mayor to see if they would be a good fit.

Giving a Speech

The mayor often shares information about important decisions that they have made in the form of a speech. In big cities, this speech might even be played on TV! It's important that the mayor thinks carefully about what they would like to say.

Exciting Events

Being a mayor isn't all meetings and decisions, though! The mayor also gets to attend many fun events, or activities, such as the openings of new buildings, dinners to help different groups, and even events at schools!

A Position of Power

As you can see, being the mayor comes with a lot of **responsibility**. Luckily, a mayor works closely with many other people. They have help when deciding what is best for the people who live in the city or town where they work!

21

GLOSSARY

communication: telling your ideas or feelings to someone or a group, often by talking to them

department: one of the major parts of something

elect: to choose someone for a job or position by voting

hire: to choose someone for a job

interview: to meet with someone to see if they would be a good person to do a certain job

resident: someone who lives in a particular place

responsibility: something a person is in charge of

transportation: the act of moving people or things from one place to another

FOR MORE INFORMATION

BOOKS

Eggers, Dave. *What Can a Citizen Do?* San Francisco, CA: Chronicle Books, 2018.

Manley, Erika S. *Mayors.* Minneapolis, MN: Jump!, 2018.

WEBSITES

Local and State Governments
jr.brainpop.com/socialstudies/government/localandstategovernments/
This website has a helpful video and activities that give information about different types of government.

Meet a Mayor: A Community Club Activity
www.scholastic.com/teachers/activities/teaching-content/meet-mayor-community-club-activity/
This interactive book features a mayor describing what he does at his job.

Publisher's note to educators and parents: Our editors have carefully reviewed these websites to ensure that they are suitable for students. Many websites change frequently, however, and we cannot guarantee that a site's future contents will continue to meet our high standards of quality and educational value. Be advised that students should be closely supervised whenever they access the internet.

INDEX

attending events 18

communication 8

departments 4, 8, 14

fire department 4

getting elected 6, 8

hiring 14

interviewing 14

laws 12

making decisions 4, 12, 14, 16, 18, 20

meetings 8, 10, 18

police department 4, 8

residents/people who live in the town 10, 20

sharing information 16

speeches 16

transportation department 8